Morning Glories
and
Moonflowers

John Eudy

For every mother and father who has had to bury a child, may you find reassurance in those who still surround you, peace in the sanctifying beauty of creation, and comfort in Our Blessed Lord.

Contents

Chapter 1: The Loss

A well-built, rustic log cabin sits at the end of a country road on the outskirts of the burgeoning town of Fort Myers, Florida. The moss has just started growing on its wood-shingled roof. A light trail of smoke rises out of the stone chimney on the left side of the house, while small green shoots have broken through the recently tilled soil in the garden on the right side. An early spring breeze blows, and the Spanish moss sways in an old oak tree out front.

Two little girls sit with their father on the front porch in front of the closed front door. Six-year-old Jamilla is nestled under her father's right arm while ten-year-old Dorinda leans on his left shoulder. Both wear plain brown dresses and are barefoot. Dorinda has her tightly curled black hair pulled back and down into two tiny braids on both sides of her head. Jamilla's loose woolen hair has not yet grown long enough to style and is a little wilder and unkempt. Their father, a strong, weathered man in his early thirties, is clean-shaven and keeps his hair short, reminiscent of his days in the army. He wears his favorite overalls, a long-sleeved denim shirt, and sturdy brown boots. They all stare off toward the

South Florida sunset, desperately seeking tranquility in the pastel twilight colors.

Any other Friday evening, the girls would be swinging their legs and giggling under the orange, pink, and purple sky while Momma and Papa sat beside each other, holding hands and discussing their day's experiences. This evening, though, the painful sounds of childbirth, which pierce the solid log walls of their little cabin, have them worried. Jamilla looks up at her father. The screams confuse and concern her. "Papa, is Momma awright?"

"Yeah, Papa," Dorinda clutches her father's right arm. "I never heard her yell like that 'fore. I'm worried."

"It's gonna be okay, girls," their father reassures. "Doc Howard and his missus are takin' care of Momma." He pauses. "She'll be givin' birth any time now. 'Fore yuh know it, that li'l one will be runnin' 'round here for you tah chase." He offers a smile, but deep down, he, too, is worried. He's never heard his beautiful wife wail like this, either. In his heart, he knows something is wrong. He pulls his daughters in close to reassure them. As soon as he does, he hears rushed steps behind him, and the door swings open. He looks over his shoulder at Mrs. Howard, the nurse, and the midwife who has blood splattered on her white apron. He holds his girls close, keeping them from seeing the red stains on her apron.

"Come quick, Samuel," she prompts before returning quickly to her post inside the cabin.

"Dorinda," Samuel's heart beats faster, "you an' your sister can't see this. I want you tuh take yer sister fer a stroll. Why don'tcha go down to the picnic field 'n see if the sea grapes are a bloomin'? Don't wander far, though, y'hear?"

"Okay, Papa," she says with slight fear. "We'll go down there 'til dark an' then come home." Dorinda gently takes her little sister's hand while her father jumps to his feet and rushes into the cabin, closing the door behind him. "C'mon Jamilla, Papa'll help take care o' momma." The two girls saunter westward down the road, each dragging their feet in the sandy wagon ruts.

They don't have to walk far before coming to the little family picnic field on the left side of the road. A few slash pines and live oak trees grow in a semi-circle around the field. The orange needles from the pines blanket the ground around short, spotty green grass clusters popping up in the sand. Sabal palms, young sea grape trees, and other small shrubs dot the undergrowth. Their dad always thought it a beautiful spot and left the field untouched when he cleared the land to build their cabin at the end of the road. The family often brought a blanket and had picnic lunches under the shade of the trees, especially when the sea grapes were ripe. However, the girls are surprised to find a stranger in their field today.

A man is kneeling near one of the oak trees in the back of the alcove. The girls stop to stare at him out of both fear and curiosity. Jamilla reaches for the security of her big sister's hand. Without looking at them, the man says, "Peace be upon you, girls. I mean you no harm, little ones."

"What're you doin' here, mister?" Dorinda cautiously inquires.

The man stands and turns to see them. He is tall and of considerable stature. He wears old dark-gray pants, brown boots (like their father's), and a lightly soiled but still white shirt with a light blue waistcoat over it. He removes his brown hat and holds it against his chest with his right hand. His facial features are unique; the girls cannot tell if he is white, black, or Seminole. His hair is dark brown and wavy, a little long, just about to touch his shoulders. He offers a beautiful smile and a nod before announcing. "My name is Præsidiel, but you can call me Mr. Ray." He returns the hat to his head. "I received word of something terrible happening and came to help. I hope you do not mind me being here; I was planting some very special flowers in your pretty little field." He motions toward two tiny green sprouts sticking out of the sandy soil. "Now, may I ask what you two are doing here this late in the day?"

Dorinda hesitates, but eventually, her childish innocence overtakes her apprehension, and she says, "Our momma is havin' a baby, but I don't think things're are a goin' well from all the yellin' that is. It sounds like she's in terrible pain."

"Yes. Yes, I know." Mr. Ray says with a sad look on his face. "However, I had hoped planting these flowers might bring your whole family peace one day very soon." He kneels back down by the little green shoots. The girls inch closer to inspect them in the twilight. "You ever heard of moonflowers?" He asks.

Ever the bold one, Jamilla says proudly, "No, sir. But Momma an' Papa call us their li'l mornin' glories. You know, just like them li'l blue flowers."

Mr. Ray chuckles. "Well, I believe your momma and papa have picked the right nickname for you two beautiful young ladies. These here are special flowers, though a little rarer. They are found only in this country of yours and are native to the southern area where you live. When they grow up, their leaves will be shaped like hearts. Their buds will open in the evening, and their supple white flowers will reflect the light of the moon itself."

He stands slowly and turns to look closely at the girls. "Now, I have a favor to ask of you. Would you two be willing to help me feed and grow these flowers?"

There is a brief awkward silence before Dorinda says, "Mr. Ray, I'm not sure our papa would want us talkin' to a stranger. 'Sides, even if we did help, what could we do to feed 'em?" Dorinda asks.

"Well, now, that is pretty simple." Mr. Ray smiles with delight. "I will return in two weeks. If you come out and see me, I will show you a special trick to make these flowers grow big. *But*," he emphasizes, "you each have to bring a clear bottle when you return. Do not worry, though. The good doctor will leave at least two medicine bottles at your house. Medicine for your momma, as it were. When those bottles are finally empty, please wash them and bring them when you return. I will show you the rest of the process then. What do you think? Can you do that?"

"I guess we can," Dorinda replies somewhat hesitantly. "Whadda we tell our papa though?"

"Well," Mr. Ray pauses, "I know this will sound strange to you, young ladies, but I need you to keep these flowers secret until the time comes. This will be the only secret I ever ask you to keep. Their growth needs to be hidden from your momma and papa until the time is right. You must not worry, though. I promise no harm will come to you as we work, and when they are ready to bloom, I also promise they will bring healing and much joy to your whole family."

The night sky settles in, and the girls hear their father calling out to them from down the road. "Dorinda! Jamilla! Where you girls at?"

"Oh. You hear that? Your papa is calling you home. It is time to go. Go on, scoot." Mr. Ray shoos them away with his hand but then waves at the girls as they run back down the road to their dad.

Samuel meets them on the road, halfway between the alcove and the cabin. He kneels, sets his lantern on the ground, and then opens his arms to greet the girls. He scoops Jamilla up with his left arm and then places his right arm around Dorinda, squeezing her shoulders and kissing her forehead. He leans down to pick up his lantern. "It's gettin' dark out here, and there ain't no moon." Turning back to the cabin, he says, "Let's get on home."

"Papa," says Dorinda, pointing toward the picnic field, "there's a man down in the field. Said his name was Mr. Ray. He's a nice man an' was friendly tuh us."

"What!" Samuel wheels around quickly. He holds the lantern above his head and peers down the road toward the field. His light shines down the tree-lined road, which appears like a long tunnel in the growing darkness. There is no movement, no sound, nor any light. He sets Jamilla down and gently moves them behind him with his free hand. He walks cautiously down to the edge of the field. He shines the lantern light around but finds no one in the alcove.

Dorinda, following close behind, speaks up, "Honest, Papa. He was here."

Samuel turns to look at his daughters. "Come on, girls. Let's git home quickly. It's a bad night." Not only does he suffer exhaustion and sorrow, but now a tinge of worry has been added. He feels some anxiety over a mysterious stranger hanging around their land.

On the way back, Samuel feels he must prepare his daughters for what is to come, so he tells them that Momma gave birth to twin girls. They look up at him with excitement but are taken aback by the tears sneaking out of the corner of his eyes. They have never seen their papa cry before, and it creates a sense of deep concern in their young hearts.

"What's the matter, Papa?" Dorinda asks with growing concern. "Are the babies okay? Is Momma okay?"

Although he has always been genuinely forthright with his daughters, Samuel hesitates before answering. He draws a deep breath and exhales. "No, darlin', they're not. There was an accident, an' yer baby sisters are gone."

"Whaddaya mean 'gone,' Papa?" the inquisitive Jamilla asks. She, too, looks concerned and fearful. Dorinda knows what it means; her eyes fill with tears, and she turns her gaze toward the ground.

Samuel stops at the end of the road several feet in front of their house, which is quiet now. He squats down and sets the lantern on the ground. He gathers his girls around the light. Fighting back his own emotions and tears, he says softly, "Yer momma gave birth tuh twin baby girls. Sadly, yer baby sisters died after they was born."

Both girls begin to sniffle.

"Momma got hurt too, but the doctor is mendin' her up. Don't choo worry now. She'll get better in time." He gently places a hand on each of their cheeks, wiping the tears away with his thumbs. He looks deep into their chestnut eyes. He gets that sting in his nose, and his eyebrow twitches as he struggles to keep the tide of emotions at bay. "We're enterin' some dark days, an' it's gonna hurt a bit, girls, but papa needs yuh tuh be strong. Ah'm gonna need yer help over the next few days, y'understand?"

Dorinda sniffles as she wipes the tears away on her sleeve. "I unnerstand, Papa. I'll try."

He looks at little Jamilla, who is speechless; the corner of her eyes and mouth are turned downward, and her eyes are full of water. "Jamilla, Ah need you tuh love on Momma for me, 'kay? Can yuh do that for me?" He asks softly.

"I try, Papa. I try," she manages to answer through the sobs.

Cupping his hands, Samuel gently pats them on their heads and pulls them both to his chest. He hugs them warmly, reluctantly letting them go after a minute. "We'll get through this, girls.

Ah promise. Never forget, Ah love yuh both with my whole heart." He picks up Jamilla with his left hand and his lantern with his right. He swings the lantern around Dorinda's shoulder. "Now let's git home."

When they enter the house, Samuel notices the crib is already gone, and almost everything has been cleared from around the bed. The young girls rush to their momma's side. She is sedated and is resting as peacefully as possible. Their father stops for a second and watches with a heavy heart as Dorinda strokes her momma's hair while Jamilla holds her hand.

Mrs. Howard quietly and discreetly finishes cleaning everything up while tending to his wife's comfort. Samuel has seen many bad things in his life, but nothing can compare to the death of his children. He stares blankly in the direction of his wife and daughters, helpless and frozen by his inability to think clearly or do anything else for them. His senses return to him after a moment. He knows some things still need to be done, so he exits back through the front door to avoid disturbing them.

He walks around the left side of the house to the back, where Doc Howard is standing by his horse and cart, head down, in solemn disbelief.

Doc has safely bundled the lifeless bodies of the family's newborn daughters in soft blankets and placed them securely in his cart. He straightens up and humbly greets Samuel as he comes near. "You've been through a lot tonight, Samuel. I want you to rest as best as you can. We'll take great care to prepare your little ones for burial and bring them back to you first thing in the morning. Right now, though, you need to take care of yourself and those lovely ladies in there. They're going to need you." Doc pauses momentarily before trying to reassure him, "Remember, my friend, God only allows us trials we can handle. Keep your faith and pray for all your beautiful girls."

With an almost indignant look, Samuel stares him in the eyes. "Ah appreciate what yuh done here t'night, Doc. You've always been good tuh me an' mah family, but Ah don't feel as though God cares much 'bout us right now."

"Now, Mr. Samuel," comes the comforting voice of Mrs. Howard from behind him. "You know that's not true." She places her soft brown hand on his shoulder as she quietly passes him. With a slight nod, he politely and humbly smiles at her as her hand slides off his shoulder. "We know you're a good man, a good husband, and a good father in the sight of God," she says softly as her husband helps her climb into the cart. "Those girls o' yours are precious. They're takin' good care of their momma right now. I know you'll see to their and your queen's care. In the meantime, we'll pray for you all."

Samuel dips his head. "Thank yuh, Missus Howard."

He watches Doc help his wife get settled in their cart. Then Doc approaches him once more to give him a silent handshake, to reassure him as best a man can. He then turns, climbs aboard the wagon, and waves goodbye with a shake of the reigns as they depart quietly.

Samuel's eyes turn toward the soft light coming through the back door of the quiet cabin. He takes a deep breath, exhales, and murmurs, "Ah'll do what I can, I guess. Ah'll do what I can." Then, he takes his first step back toward his family.

Chapter 2: Solemnity

Though exhausted, Samuel still has trouble sleeping. He rises early the following day before the sun is up. He lights a small fire in the fireplace and, from it, his lantern. He quietly looks around the silent cabin, cherishing the peaceful slumber of his wife and daughters. It is the silence that grips him, though. The sound of babies is absent from their little cabin. It makes him feel somewhat lost, unsure of what to do next. He needs something to do with his hands.

A carpenter by trade, he heads out to the small shed behind the house, where he begins building two small coffins from some good wood he was storing. He tries to keep the noise to a minimum but knows he has woken Dorinda and Jamilla because he can smell breakfast being prepared. He is grateful for Dorinda, whom he thinks the world of. He knows she will tend to her mother and little sister while he is out.

Samuel hears the door creak open, and little footprints scuffle through the sandy grass behind him. He has finished his work. He puts down his tools and buries his pain deep inside his heart. He turns to see Jamilla standing in the early morning light. Her wild, woolen hair surrounds her soft brown face like a halo. She's staring up at him expectantly. "Mornin', Papa," she says, rubbing her eyes.

"Good mornin', mah darlin'," he says.

Jamilla instinctively raises her hands toward him. Samuel squats down, and she rushes into his arms. He picks her up and holds her to his left.

"Dorinda made beckfest, Papa," she informs. "You hungry?"

"Yes, ma'am, Ah am," he says with a smile.

"Papa," Jamilla starts, "Momma said she don't wanna get up. She's sad, an' so am I."

"Me too, young'un. Me too."

The mind of a child shifts gears so fast, though, and she asks, "Whatcha doin' out here?" Jamilla looks inquisitively over his shoulder at the simple caskets. "Whad'ya make them for?"

"Ah, now don't cha go worryin' yer pretty little head 'bout that. Ah'll tell yuh 'bout it some other time."

She turns to look her father in the eyes. He sees the deep affection in her heart and smiles. She returns his grin. Still carrying her, he starts for the cabin. "Let's go check on Momma and get somethin' tuh eat."

Dorinda has set the table and is sitting by her momma, who is still in bed when they come in.

Samuel puts Jamilla down. She scurries over to kiss Momma and then runs to sit at the table. Dorinda tells Momma she loves her and goes to the table too. Samuel pats her on the back as she passes. He then sits on the small stool next to his wife, Phiby.

"Mornin', mah queen," he says with a smile. He grabs the small plate of food Dorinda left on the floor and offers her a bite.

She shakes her head no.

"Okay, looks pretty good though. Sure I can't getcha tuh eat a little somethin'?" He asks.

Again, she subtly shakes her head no.

"Okay," he says as he gets up and gently sets the plate on the stool. "I'll leave it rahght here 'case yuh change yer mind." He leans in to give her a long kiss on her cheek before whispering, "Ah love you." Samuel walks to the table to sit with his girls.

He sits across the table from Dorinda and to the right of Jamilla. He offers a half-hearted blessing for the food, and they all eat in silence afterward. Dorinda finishes her breakfast at about the same time as her father. They watch Jamilla, who always eats slower, for a minute. Dorinda turns to her father and lovingly asks, "Papa, what're their names? Our sisters, that is."

Samuel turns his gaze from Jamilla to Dorinda. He is caught off guard by the bold question at first. Momentarily struck dumb, he glances over at Phiby. He can see a tear glistening in the early morning light as it rolls down her supple, light brown cheek. She stares through the open window, pretending to ignore the conversation. He turns back to Dorinda. "Well, darlin', Momma and Ah had a couple o' names picked out. Since they're twins, Ah guess we'll jus' give 'em each one o' the names. Jemima was the first one born, an' Sabina was second."

Tipping her head slightly in contemplation, Dorinda is happy with the names. She smiles at her papa. Jamilla, cheeks stuffed full of food, says, "Them's pretty names, Papa."

He turns just in time to see breadcrumbs fall from her mouth to the floor as she speaks. Samuel can't help but shake his head and chuckle at her. "You're a mess girl."

He turns back to look at Dorinda. He reaches across the table, caresses her face with his right hand, and says, "Ah love you, mah daughter. Yer a sweet girl, yuh know that?"

She leans into his hand before he slowly pulls it back. He gets up from the table. "Ah still have a lot o' work tuh do though. You take care o' your momma for me?"

"Yes, Papa. I'll do mah best."

"Whatta 'bout me?" Jamilla asks, also wanting her father's attention.

Samuel walks behind her and then, kneeling to her right, places his left hand gently on her shoulder. He leans in with a serious but loving look and asks, "Will you be a big girl an' help yer sister for me? Help her clean up and take care o' Momma too?"

"Yessir," she says confidently with a smile.

"That's mah good girl." He cups the back of her head and kisses her forehead. He then stands back up and looks at his oldest. "Dorinda, don't forget. The goat needs milkin', and you'll need tuh tend to them chickens too. Okay, darlin'?"

"Okay, Papa."

Samuel walks back over to Phiby and gives her a peck on the cheek. She offers no reaction to his kiss, which saddens him. He turns and heads out the back door. He collects the caskets and a few tools from the shed and then walks to the picnic field. He sets everything down, sighs deeply, and looks around. *Such a beautiful place. Sure hate tuh turn it into a graveyard.* He thinks sadly; *ah guess these babies deserve the best restin' spot*

Ah can give 'em, though. He picks up his shovel and breaks ground on the left side of the alcove, close to the back. "Man, ground is always hard. Ah'm always amazed at how hard diggin' is 'round here!" He mutters to himself. He works to make a grave deep enough to hold both caskets but not so deep as to run into the waterline.

After a while, he eventually finishes. He climbs out and rests for a minute on the small mound of sandy dirt piles. Breathing heavily, he wipes the sweat from his brow and then leans on his shovel. The sight of the grave triggers a memory from his youth.

In his mind, he feels he is ten years old again. It's only been a few days since he was taken from his mother and sent to a plantation further south. He remembers feeling like an unwanted burden the first few days. At night, he curled up alone in the dirt corner of an unfamiliar shack. He is acutely aware of many strange noises in the darkness of night—creaking boards, tree limbs rustling and rattling outside, shadows passing by the cracks in the door and shutters. He wonders what makes those shadows and from which direction he might be attacked. Sambo, as he was known then, keeps watch until exhaustion finally carries his youthful mind off to sleep. Most nights, his thoughts dwell on his mother; he finds hiding tears in the darkness easier. Early on, he would cry himself to sleep, wondering what his future holds. It isn't long before he is taken in by the other slave families, though, and he begins to make new acquaintances as he works.

Weeks have passed since his arrival. It is the heat of the day; he's sweating profusely, making the dirt stick to his bare arms. Sambo is one of three boys; he's still getting to know the other two. They're digging a grave in the root-filled soil on the edge of the plantation. No crops could be grown in that wooded area, so the owner set it aside as a slave cemetery. None of the adults are allowed to stop working until nightfall either, so the boys know they not only have to dig the grave but also have to build a casket out of whatever scrap wood they can find, blacken it with shoe polish, and then get the body placed in it before the field workers come back. Samuel still remembers the rope burns on the man's neck and the stink of his dead flesh when they placed his body in the shoddy casket. Memories he never could quite shake.

Later that night, the rest of the slaves gather in the unmarked cemetery. Yellow torchlight flickers under the now dark, leafy canopy. This is the only time, in the dead of night, slaves are allowed to bury their deceased. It was also one of the extremely rare occasions when all of them could come together at the same time without the owners or overseers. So many emotions ebbed and flowed on such an occasion, from deep sorrow at the death of one of their own to the peace and relief of being able to speak freely without the overseers watching and listening. It was a valuable opportunity for Sambo to learn more about his new kin and their efforts to provide some dignity for their loved ones before their spirits moved on.

He remembers listening to the adult slaves' whispers that night about the man who was to be buried, how he was one of three who had tried to escape to the North where they could be free. All three were recaptured, however. He learns how the slave patrols are concentrated along the northern borders and the coast, making escape a risky venture. The man they were burying had been singled out as having planned the escape and subsequently hanged as an example to the others. That's also why the boys were tasked with digging the grave and preparing the body; it was meant to serve as a warning to them as well.

Young Sambo listens intently and observes the adults. He sees the brokenness of their wills, so many subdued and resigned to their condition. He knows deep down it's wrong. He knows he and they are destined for something better. The fire in his belly grows. He wants to escape, to be free to make his own way in life. Ever the courageous boy, he commits himself to never giving in to the brokenness and despair slavery has wrought. He remembers deciding that very night to find a way to be free and begins to plot his escape southward.

Now, as a free man, he sits on a pile of dirt, sand, and shells, carving the names of his infant daughters into the cross-shaped marker he made for them. In his youth, slaves were buried without markers; he resolved that his daughters would not suffer such indignation. They would be buried in a beautiful spot, and their names would be seen and remembered. Deep in contemplation about this and many other things, Samuel never notices the two new vines growing at the base of the oak trees in the back of the alcove as he carves his daughters' names into a wooden cross.

* * * * *

It's late morning. The warm spring sun has risen pretty high in the light blue sky. Finished with his work, Samuel removes his wide-brimmed hat, wipes the sweat from his brow with his kerchief, and exhales. He blows the curled wooden slivers away and takes a moment to examine his work. *That's good.* He thinks with satisfaction. Then, he hears Doc Howard's cart coming up the road. *Good timin'. Guess I shoulda 'xpected it, though. Doc's always been a good man.* He recalls serving with him in the army.

Although he was a white man from the North, Doc was the only officer besides the commanding officer who would come around often to check on the condition of the men. Doc was the only one who seemed to care about them. Samuel once asked him why he cared so much and still remembers his answer, "I believe what the founders knew to be true. That all men are created equal in the eyes of God. Because of that, I intend to provide you the same care I would anyone else. Moreover, I not only admire your courage to fight for your freedom but, well, let's just say I have a personal interest in caring for your people as well."

It was not until after the war ended, when Mrs. Howard, a free black woman, traveled South to be with her husband, that Samuel finally understood what he meant by "having a personal interest." With her assistance, Doc continues his profession as a civilian now, caring for all who call upon him.

Samuel rushes out to wave him down as he rides up. He directs him to pull his cart into the little field. "Ah'm glad Ah caught'cha, Doc," he says. "Now we kin take care o' things an' not disturb the girls up at the house."

Dr. Howard nods in agreement and then turns his cart around in the field so the back is toward the open grave. He hops down, ties off his horse's reins to a nearby tree, and then goes to the rear of the cart to properly greet Samuel.

Together, they then gently remove and place each baby into their tiny caskets. Samuel's heart sinks when he picks up Sabina. Both girls are wrapped in white swaddling and smell of flowers. Though her supple cheeks are pale and cold to the touch, she feels so good in his arms. He stalls, rocking her back and forth for a moment and patting her little butt, which rests in the palm of his strong left hand. He hasn't held them since the previous night and takes a moment to spend time with her. *Mah God, Ah wish Ah could hear 'em cry again. Jus' one more time*, he thinks.

Doc stands aside quietly, respectfully watching a loving father whom he knows Samuel to be. His heart breaks again for him as he watches Samuel finally kneel, gently place her in the casket, and then repeat his slow transition from the cart to the coffin with Jemima.

Samuel turns to Doc Howard, thanking him for taking such good care to prepare his baby girls for burial. He knows his wife helped and asks him to thank Mrs. Howard too. "Don't know what Ah'd do without y'all."

"It's the least we could do, Samuel," Doc replies somberly. "The very least."

He names each child before he nails their caskets shut. Doc then helps him carefully lower the coffins into the open grave. They gently remove the lowering ropes and then stand in silent reverence at the foot of the open grave. Both men have their hands clasped together in front of themselves in silence. After a few minutes, Doc Howard peeks at Samuel, whose furrowed brow and tear-stained face gazes downward. "You want to say something for them, Samuel?"

He slowly moves his head from side to side. "Ah don't rightly know what tuh say, Doc."

"May I?" his friend asks.

Samuel nods his head in approval.

Doc prays with a slow, steady cadence, "Lord God, heavenly king, we commit these young girls to your eternal love. Keep them safe in your mighty arms and grant them peace. Please help us understand this sorrow and strengthen us with hope. Help this family overcome their sadness. Give them confidence that little Jemima and Sabina are in a better place with you. May our Lord Jesus welcome them into his arms and bless them abundantly. Amen." He reaches over and pats Samuel on the shoulder, trying to reassure him.

"Thanks, Doc," is all Samuel can say. He sniffles, wipes the tear from the corner of his eye, and grabs his shovel. He stands by the pile of dirt and sand, ready to close the grave.

"Anything else the missus or I can do for you and your family right now?" Doc Howard asks.

"No, sir, not really," Samuel answers. "Doc, I...I 'preciate whatcha've done for us. I can't thank yuh enough."

Doc Howard looks him in the eyes. "You need anything, anything at all, brother, you just ask."

"Thank yuh, sir," Samuel affirms.

Doc nods at Samuel and pats him on the shoulder one more time. He then climbs somberly back up in his cart. Looking over his shoulder, he says, "I'll send the missus 'round after church tomorrow to check on Phiby."

Samuel nods in gratitude. "Much obliged."

Doc Howard nods back, gives the reigns a light snap, and slowly rolls out. Samuel looks down into the grave one last time, hesitating to fill it in. He reluctantly begins his toil anyway. Something about the sound of soil hitting the wooden caskets drives home the finality of their short-lived lives, but he doesn't stop shoveling until it's finished.

Once he's done, he drives the cross into the ground at the head of the grave with the shovel and then steps back to the foot of it. Samuel pauses for a moment, not just to catch his breath either. A trace of slight bitterness and anger settled upon him. He raises his eyes to the clear blue sky overhead. "You let 'em separate me from mah mother when Ah was a boy. Now I too must be separated from mah children?" he argues with God. "Ah thought Ah was a free man now, an' things were supposed tuh be better. I don't understand this, Lord. I jus' don't. What'm Ah supposed to do now?"

He listens for a response, but no answer comes. The only sound is the wind blowing gently through the Spanish moss. He lowers his head in the quiet alcove. Samuel lets out a somewhat disappointed sigh before picking up his hat and heading back to the cabin with his shovel in hand.

* * * * *

Sunday comes and goes silently. No one does much of anything. Phiby stays in bed all morning. The girls clean the cabin, cook dinner, and tend to their momma before walking to the river to pick flowers. Samuel feeds and brushes their horse, Micco. He knows it's selfish to leave all the household chores to his girls, but he needs some time to be alone with his thoughts. As he brushes Micco, he recalls the day they got him and how Phiby named him after one of the last Seminole chiefs to leave Florida.

Though sad, he allows himself a passing smile, especially when thinking of his beautiful queen. He cleans and prepares the wagon and tools before milling about the garden. There is some small satisfaction in watching their crops grow. He checks the lima beans, collard greens, corn, okra, and tobacco growing there. Gently touching the young leaves, Samuel quietly mumbles, again questioning God why he would allow this tragedy.

His thoughts are scattered, random, and fleeting. Though he is an intelligent and highly skilled man, deep philosophy is not his strong suit. He would much rather work with his hands and fix what needs fixing. Unfortunately, he finds the death of children to be something he cannot *fix*. He is eager to return to work on Monday. Being busy with his hands will give him the time to sort through his thoughts. He knows he can solve problems, build structures, and work out his feelings as a man should—with his hands. At home, the girls' emotions need repair, and he is unsure how to mend Phiby's pain and despair or how to teach Dorinda and Jamilla to understand what has happened.

Mrs. Howard visits later that afternoon. Samuel takes the girls out to sit on the porch, giving her privacy to conduct her physical checkup on their momma. She emerges out onto the porch after several minutes. He sends the girls back inside so he and Mrs. Howard can have a private conversation out by her horse.

"Samuel, I'm worried," she begins.

He has removed his hat and is slowly spinning it around by the brim in his hands. "'Bout what, ma'am?"

"Well, she's already begun healing physically, and that's good." She pauses. "But, Samuel, I've never seen a broken spirit like she has in her. I'm afraid it'll take a small miracle to bring her back."

There is a long silence. "Well, Ah guess me an' the girls have our work cut out fer us then 'cause we can't jus' give up on her."

"Oh, Samuel"—she places her hand on his shoulder—"my heart goes out to you all. I know you love her and that you'll all do your best. I'll continue to check in as often as I can, and I'll continue to pray for you every day, too."

"Thank you, ma'am." He places his hat back on his head, unties the reigns of her horse from the post on the porch, and holds the bridle while she mounts her steed. She touches him on the shoulder and offers a final, reassuring smile. Samuel hands her the reigns as she does. She sits upright in the saddle, tugs at the reins to turn her horse, and departs. Samuel waves farewell.

* * * * *

Much to his restrained delight, Monday morning has come. Samuel is both reluctant and happy to depart for work—reluctant to leave his family but eager to put his hands to familiar work. He kisses Phiby goodbye, though she doesn't respond. He reminds his girls of their chores and then kisses them each on the forehead before climbing up on his old wooden wagon. He gives the reins a light snap. "C'mon, Micco, let's go." Micco knows the road into town well. He plods along the sand-and-shell road.

A little way down the road, the rhythm of the wheels, the rattle of tools in the back, and the bounce of the seat lull Samuel into a sort of trance. He's haunted by a sense of uncertainty and fear, which causes his thoughts to slip back to the time of his escape, another time of fear and uncertainty.

He remembers how young he was, only fourteen, when he took flight to Seminole territory in the South. The mix of sun and shade on his face triggers eerie memories of the light of the full moon moving through the trees. Unlike his current trek into town, he remembers staying off the roads then but close enough to them to know if he was being hunted.

His food had run out two days into his escape. He was fighting exhaustion while keeping himself moving in a southern direction. Samuel had just crested a low hill and lumbered into a shallow, misty valley. His destination uncertain and his mind numb from fatigue, he pressed on with a dogged motivation. Rather unexpectedly, his mind sharpened, and his senses came alive. He stopped in his tracks and looked around. He suddenly realized there was no sound, no breeze, nothing. He became keenly aware there was something wrong in that valley. A knot formed in the pit of his stomach, and the hair on the back of his neck stood up. The still and silent night air had a palpable sense of evil. He listened for the sounds of men moving through the underbrush but heard nothing. No man, no beast, no nothing. His heart pounded, and his senses were heightened. "Mah Lord, mah Lord," he cried quietly, "lead me tuh safety. Please protect me, mah savior."

He began to walk again, quickly this time. Then, paralleling his own, the soft sound of steps crunching leafy grass came from the hushed woods. He knew someone or something was walking with him, watching. The blood drained from his extremities, and his skin turned cold with fear. He clambered up the next hill. The footsteps continued. He turned to look, straining his eyes to see anything or anyone, but could see nothing. Though it posed a significant risk, Samuel descended the hill into a tall grassy meadow. He was exposed now, out in the open.

Still, the hushed footfall matched his own, and he still saw nothing around him. Profoundly disturbed and filled with dread, he continued.

This went on for a half-mile before he caught the smell of burning wood mingling with the thin veil of mist closing in on him. He spotted the orange glow of a small campfire in the distance. Samuel was almost at a full run in a near panic as he moved toward the firelight. He desperately wanted more time to inspect who might be there as he feared being chased into a trap. Then, as he drew near the camp, the footsteps behind him ended, and the low mist retreated.

He paused near the wood line to get a better look at the camp's residents. They were not white, nor did they dress like anyone he had seen before. *They must be Seminole*, he thought to himself. He approached as quietly as possible, but it was not enough. The two men sitting by the fire quickly spotted him as he neared. They jumped to their feet. One drew a tomahawk from his belt, and the other his rifle. Samuel raised his hands chest high so they could see he was unarmed. He approached slowly, cautiously. The orange light flickered in his eyes and on the palms of his hands. The two lowered their weapons. He stopped well away from their campsite. Not knowing if they would understand him, he politely asked if he could join them.

Samuel was pleasantly surprised and relieved to find out they spoke broken English. The men immediately recognized he was an escaped slave; Samuel was not the first they had ever encountered. They put away their weapons and invited him to sit at their fire. Samuel never forgot their incredible generosity in feeding him or their willingness to help him go South into free lands. As he traveled South with them and other Seminoles over the next two days, he learned about the legend of Stikini, an evil witch who could turn himself into a grotesque owl man. Samuel always wondered silently if Stikini was stalking him that night.

The two men and their tribe helped Samuel escape to Fort Myers, where he lived as a refugee. He continued to learn and develop his skills as a carpenter's apprentice there. The Civil War broke out a few short months after his arrival. He frequented the Union trading post, making friends with pioneers, ranchers, and some of the remaining Seminole who came to trade. In his off time, he found those who would teach him how to ride a horse, among many other things a slave would usually never be allowed to learn. As soon as he was of age, he enlisted in the 2nd U.S. Colored Infantry, garrisoned in Fort Myers in the latter parts of the war.

As he travels into town, he reflects on the one-day battle for the fort in 1865. In the recesses of his mind, he can still hear orders being screamed, cannon fire ringing out, and the smell of gunpowder, which billowed from their rifles, lingering in the air. He remembers losing a friend on the march to Natural Bridge and another in the short-lived battle there. Though it still compounds his current sorrow, that sadness is different. They were all men, fighting and dying for their freedom. Jemima and Sabina, however, were innocents, incapable of fighting for their own lives.

Samuel remembers being mustered out of service in 1866 after the war ended. Several of his brothers-in-arms moved back to the Fort Myers region as pioneers and homesteaders, eager to live free to make a life for themselves. Those were exciting times. The prospects of working for themselves, finding a wife, marrying, and building families thrilled them. While some of his friends settled on Sanibel Island, in Punta Gorda, and even all the way out in Alva, Samuel preferred the relative safety and familiarity of the Fort Myers area. Once there, he sought out old friendships among the tiny handful of Seminole who had remained, farmers, ranchers, and others he had easily connected with before. As the area began to settle, he found much work as a carpenter. Samuel partnered with many settlers, business owners, and even the ranchers north of the Caloosahatchee River. He helped them build homes and shops in the growing communities. In turn, they helped him with his cabin. He remembers how good it felt to see so many unite in the spirit of freedom to build their towns and neighborhoods.

Micco snorts and shakes Samuel from his reflections as he nears town. He passes a young lady walking with a gentleman on the side of the road. He tips his cap, greeting them as he passes. The young lady offers him a smile, and his thoughts immediately turn to Phiby. During the construction of his cabin, one of the remaining Black Seminole men, accompanied by his oldest daughter, came to help. He and Samuel worked hard that morning before taking lunch in the lush, shady field down the road from where their cabin now sits. Sitting in the breeze, Samuel listened to the elder's stories about how his people had moved South many moons after the attack on Angola. Although he endeavored to be a polite student, Samuel could not take his eyes off Phiby; her allure was intoxicating. They exchanged bashful glances and smiles between bites and stories. His heart would beat fast each time she spoke. There was no denying their instant connection, and they fell in love that very day.

Though Samuel doesn't smoke, he plants and continues to grow a small amount of tobacco on his modest farm to offer trade with her father. It was partly through this trade that he was able to court Phiby. In addition, he gained much from her father's knowledge of hunting, foraging, identifying medicinal plants, and learning the best crops to grow. This made the hardships of frontier life easier and helped him win his bride's hand, his queen.

He still goes hunting with his Seminole brothers while their wives visit Phiby, and their children play together. He knows he can call on them in this time of need. For now, though, there is still so much to do in town and at home. Though he thinks of his girls often, Samuel loses himself in the day's toil, trying to forget the pain and worry they are all going through.

* * * * *

At home, Jamilla helps clean the house by sweeping and putting things away. Dorinda cooks and brings medicine to her momma. They both sing sweet songs to her while they prepare her breakfast. They help her to the table, where she sits and stares out of the only window in the house. After breakfast, the girls clean up, and then Dorinda does her best to teach Jamilla what she knows about reading and writing. In the afternoon, they feed the chickens and tend the goat. They work in the garden for a bit. The fresh sea-blown breeze stirs the Spanish moss in the surrounding trees, and warm sunshine feels good on their soft brown faces.

Once their chores are done, the girls' curiosity gets the best of them, and they sneak off to the field. They approach the freshly covered grave slowly. Except for the breeze and occasional birdsong, it is quiet. The girls stop at the foot of the grave and stare. For both, there is something amiss about the appearance of the grave. Having witnessed the birth of her little sister, Dorinda can feel the loss. She remembers the crying, the feeding, and the cleaning when Jamilla was a baby. The absence of her newborn twin sisters makes her heart feel heavy; she is unsure how to express it. She reads the names on the cross out loud for Jamilla, who sees her big sister's reaction but is otherwise confused. She empathizes with her yet doesn't truly understand or know how to react to everything that has happened.

* * * * *

Phiby is alone. The girls have gone outside, and Samuel is working in town. She gets up from the table and goes to lie on her side in bed. Still in pain from childbirth, she holds her stomach as she walks. It's not just the physical pain that hurts either, but the deafening silence stings her heart and mind. There are no infant cries, no tiny child to nurse or care for. There is no newborn-baby scent other parents enjoy. This was supposed to be a happy time, yet her joy has been stripped away. She feels utterly alone and useless.

As the desolation sinks deeper into her heart, a wicked voice whispers in her ear, "You failed. You are not a good wife. You are not a good mother or daughter."

Phiby cries. Tears roll down her cheek onto her pillow. "Yes, Ah am," she argues weakly.

"There is not a single person who will understand your failure, your pain. You are alone."

"That's not true," she murmurs to herself. "Samuel…Mah father…Dorinda an' Jamilla."

"They are not here. They do not understand. They will not forgive."

"Yer wrong." Phiby curls up in a ball. Her face contorted with both pain and sadness. "They still love me." She pulls the blankets up to cover her mouth. "Go 'way, evil spirit. Leave me be."

The voice is silent, but the damage is done. Phiby begins to think about what could have been. *If only Ah had known they was twins. What if they had lived? What if? What if?* She closes her eyes and cries herself to sleep.

* * * * *

Standing solemnly at the foot of their sister's grave and observing her surroundings, Jamilla is the first to point out the oddness of the scene, saying, "It s'posed to be covered wiff grass aweady?" She points at the ground with her left hand while scratching her head with her right.

Dorinda is suddenly aware that is what is amiss. "No, Ah don't think grass grows *that* fast. Kinda odd." She also begins to look around. "Look o'er there. Them flowers Mr. Ray planted are a growin' too." The two moonflower vines are already reaching for the tree trunks of nearby trees.

"Wow!" Jamilla says.

After being briefly mesmerized, Dorinda turns her attention back to the grave. Both girls stand in somber silence for a short time before Dorinda speaks up, "Papa said their tiny bodies are a restin' here, but he says their souls are up 'n heaven with God."

"That's far 'way, isn't it? You think we'll get tuh meet 'em one day?" Jamilla asks, who is innocently twisting and turning slightly as she looks around.

"I s'pose…when we get to heaven too, I guess," Dorinda answers. Reluctant to dwell on thoughts of death, she changes the subject. "We oughta be gettin' back now. Gotta check on Momma."

Jamilla nods in agreement, and both girls turn to leave. Jamilla reaches for her big sister's hand as they stroll back up the road. They return to the cabin hand in hand. There, they find their momma sleeping in her bed. The girls quietly add wood to the embers in the fireplace and stoke it into a small fire. They then begin preparing a simple dinner for Papa. They know he will be hungry after a long day's work.

* * * * *

Though the days seem short because of all his work, it feels like time is dragging slowly on. A whole week passes. Each day, Samuel goes into town for work while the girls tend to the house and their momma, who has sunken deeper into depression. Long periods of prolonged and awkward silence interrupt the family's time together. The girls do their best to care for their momma, love on her, and cheer her up. Mrs. Howard checks in on her a couple of times. She lets Samuel know that, physically, his wife is mostly healed, but she is still concerned for her emotional well-being.

During the day and some evenings, Phiby often mills about the cabin or finds her way out on the porch. Occasionally feeling adventurous, she might walk through the garden or feed the chickens, but she prefers to sit in her rocking chair by the fire. Samuel and the girls can still see she struggles mightily with the death of Jemima and Sabina. He knows she is falling into despair. She continually turns her thoughts inward, showing no energy or zest for life around her. She withdraws further and further from them. Samuel feels her anguish in his own heart. He knows he needs to do something to bring her back.

On Friday evening, after work, he takes her and the girls on a long walk to the banks of the river to look for sea grapes and flowers and watch the sunset. The time with her family does offer a temporary respite, a reassurance that they still love and cherish her, but she quickly falls back into depression the next day. Samuel must persistently show her how much he loves and needs her.

Though most of the last few nights she has said nary a word, she sometimes lashes out at them in pain and sorrow, especially when Samuel plays with the girls. This was the case on Saturday evening; her unstable emotions came out as resentful anger toward the girls. It was raining heavily outside, so the girls were inside playing, a little too noisy as children sometimes do. Samuel had cleared the table and was starting to wash up. The girl's laughter became too loud, and Phiby barked at them, threatening to send them out in the rain. Samuel quickly intervened, drawing her ire and derision.

He knows it has been a week since the tragic night and that Phiby is likely aware of this, even if unknowingly. Although painful to hear, he humbly and quietly accepts all her insults, knowing they come from a place of loss and pain.

Finally exhausted from yelling at them, Phiby shuffles over to the fireplace and plops down in the rocking chair in front of it. She slips back into her distant, silent stare. Looking for reassurance, the girls help their papa finish cleaning up from dinner. He then quietly takes them out to the front porch to watch the rain.

Samuel sits in his chair with Jamilla on his lap. She sits on his left leg, and he has wrapped his left arm around her. She nuzzles in close, resting her head on his chest and listening to his heart. Dorinda leans her back against the house. She and Papa listen to the rain falling on the porch's roof. After a few moments of peaceful contemplation, Samuel motions with his right hand for Dorinda to come closer. "Come 'ere, sweetheart." She comes round and sits on his right knee. Still holding onto Jamilla, who has popped her head up, he gently places his right hand on Dorinda's shoulder blade. "Tomorrow's Sunday, girls. Ah think we all need tuh go tuh church, so I want'cha in bed early t'nite, okay?"

"Yes, Papa." They nod in unison.

He looks into their soft chestnut eyes, and his tone softens, "Don'choo worry 'bout what yer momma said, girls. She don't mean a lick of it. She don't mean tuh ignore you either. Deep down, she still loves yuh. Ah promise. She'll be right as this rain 'fore long. You'll see. Before yuh know it, she'll be brushin' yer hair, teachin' yuh how tuh read, and a ticklin' yuh again." He pokes at Jamilla's belly to get her to giggle. He continues to reassure them. "Ah'm proud o' you, girls. Yer doin' a great job 'round here. You keep up the good work for me?"

Both girls, smiling softly, nod in agreement again before wrapping their arms around his neck, squeezing, and heading into the cabin to get ready for bed.

Samuel lingers on the porch for a spell, staring at the dark sky. Feeling he's given his daughters enough time to change into their nightgowns, he gets up and goes into the cabin to tuck them in and kiss them goodnight. He walks toward his bed, looks at Phiby curled up there, and then decides to return to the porch for a while.

He sits in his chair, watching the rain fall and wondering if he is doing the right things. He looks skyward as if seeking an answer from God, but he doesn't say a word. A bolt of lightning, buried deep in the dark clouds, flashes, illuminating them for the briefest of moments. A low rumble moves across the sky a minute later. The floor behind him creaks in the ensuing silence. Samuel looks over his shoulder to see Phiby standing in the doorway. She looks at him with a cautious melancholy. He stands up and motions to her softly. "Mah queen, please, come sit with me?"

She moves silently to the chair next to him and sits. Samuel waits for her, and then he, too, sits. He gazes at her sad face, forgetting all about the rain while she, in turn, discovers it. She looks out into the dark, rainy night. He places his hand upon hers, but she does not acknowledge him. He sees the light from another distant lightning flash on her face; a low thunder follows again. "I don't understand why God punishes me so," she whispers. "Why does he hate me?"

Samuel doesn't have an answer, but he desperately wants to reassure her. "Oh, Phiby, God doesn't hate you." He gently pats and rubs her hand. "Ah can't rightly say why he let this happen, but Ah know God cannot hate. It's not 'n his nature." Samuel pauses. "Even if we have done somethin' wrong, yuh know Ah'll always be by your side, right? Yuh know Ah'll always love you."

Phiby doesn't respond. She sits quietly, watching the rain fall into little puddles. A few minutes pass. The distant storm has moved on, and the rain softens to a light sprinkle. "Ah guess I ought to go tuh bed," Phiby mumbles as if worn out. She slowly and quietly gets up and walks into the cabin. Samuel follows her, stopping to secure the door and shutter the windows. He slips off his boots and overalls and climbs in next to her. He snuggles close, and although she keeps her back to him, she allows him to spoon a little. The sound of light rain pattering the roof quickly sends them both off to sleep.

* * * * *

The early morning Sunday sun is just beginning to peek between the gaps in the window shutters. Samuel is lying on his back in a cold sweat. He is wide awake; the nightmares that plague him from time to time have reared their ugly head again. He woke several times throughout the night, breathing heavily and frantically looking about the cabin before realizing he was only dreaming. No bullets were whizzing by him, no cannon fire exploding, and no crack of the overseer's whip. He lies there staring at the rafters, dwelling upon the tormenting dreams of his daughters being stripped from his arms of suffering and loss.

Samuel is tired; he feels empty, dazed, and confused. He wonders, returning to reality, *How could all this happen? What'm Ah supposed tuh do now?*

Bulldogged as ever, he forces himself to get up. He quietly scuffles across the wooden floor and builds a small fire in the fireplace. As silently as he can, he prepares coffee in his old metal coffee pot and sets it next to the fire. He dresses while it percolates, donning a clean white shirt, a clean pair of dark brown pants with suspenders, and his light tan waistcoat. Afterward, he pours his coffee into his little metal mug and sits at the table. First, he stares across the room at the fire, then down into his cup, and then surveys his household.

His mind slowly returns to both God and his former life. He specifically remembers the older slave who worked in the house when he was a boy. Whenever she could, she would sneak the owner's Bible out of the house in the evening and bring all the children together for a secret time of worship. She would teach them to read and write words in the dirt using sticks. A smile creeps across Samuel's face. Those memories bring him a sort of peaceful happiness. He relished those lessons. As he reminisces, he is reminded of the story of King David and Bathsheba's child who died. He thinks about how King David responded. He fasted and mourned before returning to the house of God. Samuel sees this as an example of what he must do. "Ah guess Ah oughta go tuh church too," he whispers before sipping his coffee. "Maybe, it'll get Phiby on the right path tuh healin'."

He hears blankets rustle; his girls are stirring. He sets his coffee down on the table, cupping its warmth in his palms, and watches his little ones from across the room. Dorinda rolls to her side, where she can see her papa. She slowly opens her eyes. She looks lovingly at him. Samuel smiles at her and, in a deep voice, whispers, "'Bout time yuh woke up, sleepyhead."

"Morin', Papa," she whispers back.

Jamilla unexpectedly pops up on the other side of the bed like a prairie dog. Sitting upright, she rubs the sleep from her eyes with little balled-up fists before squinting to see her papa. Her nightgown is disheveled, and her woolen hair is a mess. "Bright-eyed 'n bushy-tailed Ah see." Samuel chuckles to himself. "Welp,"—he slaps his legs—"Ah guess it's time to rise 'n shine, little mornin' glories. Gotta get tuh church t'day.

C'mon now. Put on them pretty li'l blue 'n white dresses for me."

"We will, Papa," Dorinda says with a bit of excitement. She flings the blankets back, half covering Jamilla, who exclaims louder than she should.

"Hey!" Jamilla pushes the blankets off. Dorinda gets out of bed, opens their trunk, and starts laying their clothes on the messy bed. Jamilla stretches her arms out, yawns, and again rubs her eyes, saying, "Mornin', Papa." She, too, jumps out of bed, her little bare feet pattering around the bed to where her big sister is. Both girls always love dressing up and going into town.

Samuel gets up from the table and sits on the bed next to Phiby. She is already awake and has been listening passively. "Mornin', mah queen." He gently strokes her long, loose curls. "Let's go to church this mornin'. Give our respect to the Lord."

"Ah guess." She sighs. "I jus' don't know why. I don' think he loves us no more."

Samuel leans down next to her. "Come on now, Phiby. Yuh know that's not true. He still loves us. Maybe if we go to church, he'll bless us an' heal us." Without a word, she twists to sit up next to him. He smiles at her, and she shoos him away. She gets up slowly and starts making the bed. His spirits are lifted by her willingness to get up and about. He retrieves his coffee from the table and, to give the women their privacy goes out on the front porch to finish it. Once he's emptied the cup, he goes around back to clean all his tools out of the wagon, making it presentable for his ladies. He hitches it up Micco and leads the horse and cart to the front of the cabin.

A little later, all the ladies emerge from the cabin dressed, groomed, and ready for town. They're all standing on the porch when Samuel comes around the corner. He stops Micco and the wagon and finds himself staring at them all. "Wow!" He exclaims. "Y'all are beautiful!" The girls, truly relishing their father's flattery, smile from ear to ear. They run up to the wagon, Dorinda pausing to hug her dad before jumping right up into the back of the wagon. Jamilla is right behind her. She comes with open arms. He knows she still struggles to climb in, so he scoops her up and whisks her into the back with her sister. He then turns to see his stunning bride waiting on the porch.

Samuel hasn't seen Phiby dress up for quite some time. Even after all their years together, he still looks upon her with the same breathless intoxication as he did when they met. Around the house, she usually wears a simple dress and apron with a kerchief, keeping her long curly hair behind her, and Samuel still finds her attractive in that. This morning, however, she stands on the porch in the bright sun wearing a beautiful cream-colored dress with a silky brown shawl over her shoulders. Her hair is tucked under a copper-tinted headwrap, making her smooth brown skin radiant in the sun. Indeed, he finds her most alluring.

He approaches as slowly and smoothly as possible, offering his arm to her out of gentlemanly courtesy. She takes it as she steps off the porch toward the wagon. Samuel fawns over her as they walk, using the moment to genuinely let her know how much he loves her and how gorgeous she is. "Ahh, there's mah queen." He smiles coyly at her. "You really are irresistible, yuh know that?"

She offers him a half smile that disappears as fast as it appears. He knows she's still not herself but is encouraged by her smile. He holds her hand as she climbs into the wagon and swiftly follows her. There is no denying the small joy he feels in this moment with his family heading toward the house of God.

The girls always enjoy riding in the back of their little brown wagon, giggling and pointing at things they see. That morning, Dorinda spies a Cooper's hawk staring back at them from its perch in an old oak tree near the house. She immediately points it out to Jamilla, who studies it carefully before they round the bend and are out of sight. The family enjoys a relatively silent ride with no real conversation. They go from the rutted sandy country roads to the well-laid and wide shell-ridden lanes in town. The fresh morning breezes sway the lush palms and moss-covered oaks along the way while slightly soothing their worries.

Not far from the river, sitting among the thinned-out tree line on the outer end of town is a long, simple wood clapboard church house. It sits upon short pillars, raising it above any water that might rush inland from a storm surge. Two casement windows adorn the front and back, with three more along each side. Mounted in the gable over the double-door entrance and large railed porch is an old bronze bell, pitted and faded brown with patina. A small steeple with a whitewashed wooden cross also adorns the roof above the doors. It's not a lavish building, but the congregation made it a good church.

Full of decent, God-fearing people, former slaves, soldiers, and pioneers alike, there is a true sense of community and brotherly love when they all come together. Samuel wonders if this gathering of the faithful is a small glimpse of life in heaven itself. Either way, he believes this is just what his family needs right now—to be in the house of God surrounded by people who will lift their spirits.

Upon arrival, Samuel sees his girls wave enthusiastically to friends out of the corner of his eye. He reigns Micco to a stop and then turns to see his daughters look back at him eagerly. With a smile, he nods his approval for them to jump down and play. Dorinda helps Jamilla down, and they quickly run off to spend time with the other children. Samuel jumps off the wagon. He leads the horse to a nearby hitching post and slips the reigns through the hoop. He then walks to Phiby's side and escorts her from the carriage. They arrive just in time as the preacher's son begins to pull the rope, sounding the church bell. Although nothing is said, the absence of a baby in their presence is noted by many. Still, Samuel and Phiby are greeted warmly as they enter the church. They quietly sit close to the middle, as usual. Samuel likes to sit closest to the aisle at the end of the pew. As usual, Phiby takes her place at his side and the girls to her right.

Phiby keeps her head down after they sit. She is overcome with an unjustified paranoia, feeling as though everyone stares pitifully at her, and it makes her uncomfortable. She wonders to herself, *Ah know they saw me with child. They gotta be wonderin' where the baby is. What're they thinkin' 'bout me*? An unearned sense of shame and motherly failure dominates her thoughts. She feels outside of God's grace, even in his own house.

Service begins, and the preacher reads from 1 Corinthians 10:13, 2 Corinthians 1:3–7, and James 1:12. He gives a fine sermon on trials, faith, and resiliency before reading Isaiah 65:17–25, God's promise of a new creation. Samuel senses God is speaking to him intimately. Emotions well up within his chest, but he pushes them, along with the urge to weep, down into his chest. He retains a stoic look on his face, if only for his family and the rest of the congregation. Phiby, still questioning God's reasoning for their loss and his purpose behind it all, keeps her head down during the sermon. She uses her handkerchief to wipe tears from her cheek occasionally.

The preacher asks for prayer requests. Samuel is nervous. He twists and turns slightly in his seat, unsure of himself for the first time in a long time. He wants to ask for prayers but has never been one to ask for much from anyone, especially prayer. He generally keeps his conversations with God private for the most part. Though things have changed, he knows he could use as many prayers as possible. Not necessarily for himself, mind you; he needs them for Phiby, Dorinda, and Jamilla. He waits patiently for a time when he can stand and present his request. The preacher keeps looking in his direction while surveying the congregation as if to give Samuel a sign, an acknowledgment. "Are there any more prayers?" he asks.

Samuel raises his hand. The preacher smiles at him with a gentle, fatherly smile, encouraging his bravery. He extends his hand toward him in recognition. Samuel rises to his feet, again fidgeting with the brim of his hat in front of him. In a humble voice, he says, "I know some of y'all probably already heard this, but we lost our newborn babies a week ago. They was twin girls...Jemima and Sabina." He pauses for a moment and looks down at his own family. Phiby still has her head down, but Dorinda and Jamilla look up toward him with the purest look in their eyes. "I'd like tuh ask y'all tuh pray for them and fer us. Ah'm not sure what God's plan is, but if y'all would, please pray for his guidance in our time o' need. Thank yuh." He nods at the preacher with gratitude and then sits back down. He places his hand on Phiby's leg. She is shaking. He pats her leg and gently squeezes it, trying to comfort her. Leaning back to look at his girls, he offers them a half smile.

"Amen, brother," the preacher says. He asks all to pray for their and the other congregants' requests and then continues with the remainder of the service. Afterward, Samuel and his family are met by Doc Howard, his wife, and a handful of women at the bottom of the stairs leading up to the front door. He sends the girls off to play with the other children while he meets with them. He learns that the loss of a child is far more common in his community than he ever knew. He is slightly taken aback by his unawareness that other families, friends, and neighbors have endured the same pain. Neither he nor Phiby says much in response to their stories.

Phiby stares blank-faced out at the playing children. Quiet envy grows in her heart. She is envious that she does not have her own babies, but they all have theirs. Samuel, in contrast, receives a small amount of solace, knowing they are not alone in their suffering. They chat for a short period before Phiby calls Dorinda and Jamilla back. She tells Samuel she is ready to go home. He politely excuses himself to retrieve Micco and the wagon and then helps them all in. The girls enthusiastically wave farewell to their friends as the carriage rolls away.

The ride home is again a quiet one. Samuel contemplates the scripture while Phiby falls back into her silent depression. As they pass by the field near the house where Jemima and Sabina are buried, only Dorinda and Jamilla notice the moonflower vines spreading. They look at each other with excitement and giggle with some anticipation of seeing whether or not Mr. Ray will actually return.

Chapter 3: Catchin' Moonbeams

Another week has grudgingly passed. Phiby is a little more active. She makes herself busy around the cabin, cleaning and cooking more often. When she's done, though, she usually sits at the table, gazing out the window or in her rocker near the hearth, staring at the fire. When she feels cooped up, she goes out to the garden or collects eggs from the chickens. She still doesn't interact with Dorinda and Jamilla as much as she used to. Friends from town, even a couple of the Seminole wives, visit them to check in on her and the girls, but Phiby always turns them away, telling them she's okay. Deep down, she still feels like no one could possibly relate to her struggles. Her silence and depression continue to bring worry to the whole family.

It's now the second Saturday since the babies passed. Neither Dorinda nor Jamilla has forgotten about Mr. Ray and his request. They have occasionally snuck down to the field to check on the moonflowers to see if they're growing. They have also managed to stash the two clear medicinal bottles left behind by Doc Howard out by the garden. That evening, Papa comes home, eats dinner, and rests for a spell before telling the girls, "Don't choo worry 'bout the dishes t'nite, girls. Ah'll wash 'em up. Besides, Ah'd like tuh spend some time with Momma. Go on out 'n play fer a while." He shoos them off with a wave of his hand and a smile. It's just what they wanted to hear. They bounce excitedly, running out the front door and toward the garden.

Phiby sits in her rocking chair, staring at the dancing flames in the fireplace. Samuel frequently glances at her while he cleans up the dishes. Once he's finished, he picks up a chair and sets it down to her right. He sits facing her, takes her hand, and does his best to love on her. Desperately hoping to bring her back to her old self, he whispers in her ear, reminding her of their courtship. "Mmmm...The scent of yer light brown skin. How yer copper eyes gleamed in the sunlight. Them dimples in yer soft, supple cheeks when yuh offered me that bright smile behind them full pouty lips." He tilts his head and leans in to look up into her sad eyes. He offers a smile, but she does not return it. Samuel straightens back up. "From the day Ah met yuh, Ah loved yuh. Ah loved the way yuh carried yerself, strong, independent, 'n proudly free. Yet, yuh're always humble 'n kind." He strokes her hand. "Come back tuh me, Phiby." He begs. "Come back tuh me, mah queen."

* * * * *

It's just before dusk, and it's been two weeks since Mr. Ray planted the two flowers in the field. The girls grab their bottles stashed under the big tobacco leaves in the garden and run down to see if Mr. Ray would be there. Many emotions swirl around in their little hearts and minds. Who is Mr. Ray? Can they trust him? Will he keep his promise? How exactly are they going to feed the flowers? The girls stop in their tracks as they round the corner of the field. Mr. Ray is indeed there. He is kneeling on his right knee to the side of the small marker where their sisters are buried. A small, elegant, ornate brass lantern sits near the cross and glows a soft golden color in the evening twilight. He holds his hat against his chest with his right hand while his sizeable left hand is flat, palm down, on top of the grave. He doesn't lift his head or turn around but greets them nonetheless. "Peace be upon you, young ladies."

"Hello, Mr. Ray," Dorinda says, still possessing a little mistrust in him.

"Hiya, Mista Wray." Jamilla giggles with a more trusting innocence typical of her age.

"I must admit., I am both sad and happy to be here," Mr. Ray says. "I lament your momma's misery, but I am overjoyed you remembered to come and see me." He stands gracefully, places his hat on his head, and turns to look at the young girls. Dorinda stands still with a simple smile while Jamilla twists back and forth, swinging the little bottle in front of her. "And you remembered the bottles. Excellent!" He claps his hands and presents a wide smile. "Come here and look." He points excitedly to where he planted the two flowers. They have continued to spread and grow; their twining vines are starting to reach up onto the trunks of three oak trees.

"We saw they was growin'," Dorinda states, "but they don't have any flowers on 'em."

"Well, that is why I asked you to bring those bottles. We are going to feed them," Mr. Ray says.

"Wiff what?" Jamilla asks.

"With moonbeams, Miss Jamilla," Mr. Ray answers with a wink. "We are going to fill those bottles with moonbeams, give them a kiss to add a little love, and then pour them out on the vines."

"Aww, come on now, Mr. Ray. That's impossible," Dorinda scoffs. "I never heard such a thing."

"Ooh! Magic?" Jamilla squeals before he can retort. "You gonna use magic?"

"No, not exactly," Mr. Ray says. "We are going catch the beams with God's blessing. Here, little one, bring me your bottle." He waves for Jamilla to come closer as he kneels beside the grave. She hurries to him in the already-darkening sky. A single thin beam of light shines faintly on their baby sister's grave. "See here, the half-moon's light is shining through the tops of those trees. Go ahead, hold your bottle out in the light. Open side up now so the bottle will fill up." The light shines into the glass container, illuminating it. "Father in heaven," Mr. Ray prays, "bless the light we collect. Help it nourish the flowers we have planted in honor of this loving family."

Jamilla's eyes grow big and round, beaming with excitement, as the bottle glows bright with white light. Dorinda's jaw hangs open in surprise as Mr. Ray finishes the prayer.

"Okay, put your hand over the top of the bottle and come over here." Mr. Ray directs Jamilla over to the vine. She stares at the bottle as she strolls over. "Now, give the bottle a little kiss. Show God and your baby sisters you love them."

Jamilla gives the glowing bottle a tiny peck on its side and then looks back at Mr. Ray.

"Lovely. Turn the bottle over and shake the light on this vine." He points to the one on the right. "You might need to give it a little shake or tap on the bottom, but do not drop it." He stands back and watches the beautiful wee girl turn the bottle over and, with both hands, give it a shake. A faint but sparkling white mist cascades from the bottle to the ground, covering the vine's dark green heart-shaped leaves. Then, as if the vine had absorbed it, the glowing mist slowly disappears.

Jamilla watches until the twinkling lights are gone, then looks up at Mr. Ray when nothing happens. He nods at her, directing her attention back to the vine, which suddenly and methodically grows a few feet up and around the tree. Her eyes light up, and taking much pride in her efforts, she dances with carefree joy.

"I told you," Mr. Ray says, laughing with her. He looks over at Dorinda, who appears to have changed her mind about feeding them and is eager to try it herself. He smiles. "You want to try it too, Miss Dorinda?"

"Oh yes, sir!" she says excitedly. She runs over to meet him near the grave. She kneeled and held her bottle out into the moonbeam like her sister. Mr. Ray repeats the prayer, and her bottle begins to glow, too.

"You know what to do, yes?" Mr. Ray asks.

"Yes, sir," Dorinda replies with humble confidence as she cautiously covers the opening with her hand.

"Let us feed the vine on the left side this time." He points to it. "Do not forget to give it a little kiss." He stands back, watches her move swiftly to the vine, and give a little *smek* to the side of her bottle. Jamilla dances over to see her big sister pour her bottle out. They again watch intently for a moment before the vine shoots up and around the other tree, just like the first. Both girls look at each other, smiling from ear to ear. They begin to giggle, then laugh, and then dance about with pure childish glee. Mr. Ray chuckles in their delight. "Okay. Now, how about you both collect some light, and we'll feed them one last time for the night."

The girls do just as they did before. Mr. Ray prays for the blessing. The girls kiss their bottles, fill the light with love and joy, and sprinkle the glittering moondust over both vines while dancing and spinning. Mr. Ray claps with rhythmic approval at their innocent merriment. "Lovely job, girls. Just lovely." The vines grow again along the ground and toward other trees.

Dorinda spins around while dancing, and the cross anchored in the ground catches her attention. Her merriment suddenly fades. She walks around to the foot of it. Mr. Ray watches silently as a slight melancholy overtakes her. She thinks about her mother, about doing her best to care for her and make her happier. She looks over her right shoulder at the visitor and says, "Mr. Ray, our momma's not feelin' well. She's really sad." Jamilla stops dancing, too, and focuses on what her big sister says. Mr. Ray motions for her to come near as he moves toward Dorinda; Jamilla follows him.

"I know little one. I know." He squats down so he can look them both in the eyes. "I promise we are going to make her better. You will see it in time. What we are doing here, these flowers we are growing, they will help. I promise. We must let things run their course right now." He pauses for a second, puts his left hand on Dorinda's shoulder, and pokes at Jamilla's belly with his right index finger, just like her papa does. He smiles and says, "I tell you what. You girls keep coming back here the next few nights, only when the weather's nice, of course, and we will get these vines to grow tall and wide. Their flowers will be ready to bloom by the full moon. If we do that, I believe it will help make things right with your momma and papa. Agreed?"

Jamilla giggles. "Yeah."

Dorinda nods her approval.

"My darling, Dorinda, do you know what your name means?" Mr. Ray inquires a little more solemnly.

"Momma tol' me once. She said it meant *gift of God*."

"She is right. You are a gift. You are a gift to your momma and your papa. You are a gift to little Jamilla here, too." He lightly pokes her belly again to make her giggle. "You have already done so many good things for them. You are a precious gift indeed. Keep your head high, young one, and keep the same joy you had for God tonight in your heart."

"Yes, sir. Ah'll do mah best." She smiles at Mr. Ray.

"Whadda 'bout me, Mista Wray? What's mah name mean?" Jamilla asks.

"Oh, well, that is an easy one. Your name means *beautiful*. And that you are, wee girl. You are beautiful inside and out."

Jamilla, holding her jar behind her back, begins twisting side to side and smiling from ear to ear with the compliment.

Mr. Ray can't help but smile with joy at her innocence. "Now, girls, it is time for you to return home. Okay? Your papa is going to start worrying about you. So go on, scoot."

"Thanks, Mr. Ray!" Dorinda shouts as the girls start toward their little house. Her apprehension about the mysterious stranger has turned into a complete trust in Mr. Ray.

"Do not forget to say your nightly prayers. You hear?" Mr. Ray hollers out. "God loves it when you say goodnight to him."

"We will," Dorinda shouts as they turn the corner and head up the road.

* * * * *

Things go nearly the same way over the next several days. Phiby, physically recovered for the most part, shuffles around the house, straightening and cooking from time to time. Dorinda and Jamilla handle routine and daily chores in the house and the garden. During the afternoon, when it gets hotter, Dorinda sits with Jamilla on the front porch, instructing her how to read and write. *Momma is a better teacher than me*, she often thinks, but still, she does her best to teach her little sister.

Each morning, Samuel hitches up his wagon, which is already loaded with his tools, and goes to work. He earns his keep and loses himself in his work, where he subconsciously sorts through his troubles. He travels by the field each day but forbids himself to look upon his infant daughters' grave when he passes. Instead, he focuses on the day's projects, keeping the flood of emotions at bay. This self-denial means he never notices the dark green vines blanketing the ground and reaching up the trunks of several trees. For him, what was once a happy place is now a place of sorrow, and he is already fighting off a growing sense of helplessness, bewilderment, and despair. He returns home in the late afternoon each day, hungry and ready to eat. After dinner, he spends a little time with his girls, who often make him laugh and smile. He then chases them off for a time so he can make an effort to woo Phiby out of her deep depression.

That is when the girls run down to the field to meet Mr. Ray. They continue feeding the spreading moonflower vines with moonbeams they catch in their jars. Much to the delight of their benevolent visitor, they also dance and sing in the warm evening air.

Chapter 4: The Gift of Sight

It's been nearly a month now since Samuel buried Jemima and Sabina. At dusk, he sits in his rocking chair on the porch, watching the yellow-orange sunlight set one side of the sky ablaze while the indigo hues rise on the opposite side. The full moon looms low and heavy in the Saturday sky. Thinking their papa was out back, Dorinda and Jamilla come bouncing out of the cabin and off the porch with their bottles in hand. They don't notice their papa sitting in his chair. Samuel, feeling like something isn't right, like they are hiding something, stops them. "Now, where do you two think yer a'goin' in such a hurry?"

They both come to a sliding stop and turn to face their papa, swiftly hiding the bottles behind them. "We're just goin' fer a walk, Papa," Dorinda says shyly.

"Whatcha got in yer hands?" Samuel asks as he stands up. He knows his girls are not capable of lying. He leans his shoulder against the post and, placing his hands in the bib of his overalls, stares down at them with a curious yet already-knowing look.

Dorinda realizes they've been found out. She's a good girl, though, a truly honest girl, and she presents the medicine bottle. Jamilla, who watches her every move, also holds her bottle out in front of her. Dorinda, eyes moving from the direction of the field to the ground in front of her, tells her papa about meeting Mr. Ray, feeding the flowers, and everything else they have been doing the last couple of weeks. Her voice rose excitedly as she told him the moon was almost full, and this was supposed to be the last night before "the surprise" Mr. Ray had planned for them all.

At first, Samuel doesn't know how to respond to such a fantastic tale. However, his thoughts quickly turn to suspicion over the idea of a stranger hanging out in the field close to their cabin. Dred rises from his stomach to his chest. He hasn't felt fear like this since his escape. He stands upright, takes his hands out of his overalls, and spins his head to look down the road. He then snaps at the girls. "Git inside. Both o' yuh." His firm tone causes them to waver for a second. Samuel turns and sees they're still standing there slack-jawed, looking at him in bewilderment. "Go on, git!" He exclaims. He jumps off the porch and points toward the door. The girls rush back inside; Jamilla starts to cry. Samuel turns to look back down the road, walking sideways up on the porch and toward the front door.

The girls are confused and scared by his sudden change in demeanor; Jamilla is whimpering. They're not used to seeing their papa upset or behaving this way. Samuel quickly closes the shudders on the window and then secures the back door. He grabs his Spencer rifle from the mantle on the fireplace, cocks the lever, loads a round into the chamber, and cautiously goes to the front door to look around.

Standing by the foot of her bed, Dorinda meekly asks, "Papa?"

"Not now, Dorinda! You'uns git over there by yer momma an' stay there." He doesn't look at the girls. Instead, his gaze is fixed down the road. He hears their feet patter across the wooden floor and then them jumping on the bed with momma. The sky outside is darkening. The full moon's brightness helps light the sandy and grassy ground while the tree line sways gently, casting shadows. Samuel neither sees nor hears any movement. He only hears the rattling palms and tree leaves in the early evening breeze. He steps back inside, closes, and locks the front door.

Phiby, restless, uncomfortable, and annoyed, sighs before getting out of bed and going to sit in the rocking chair by the fireplace. Still carrying his rifle in his left hand, Samuel approaches the girls. He squats down in front of them. Jamilla, sniffling with tears in her eyes, leaves her bottle on the bed and jumps off it. She runs to her papa, flings her little arms around his neck, and squeezes him. Samuel wraps his right arm around her and returns her hug. She lets go after a minute and, backing up, says, "I sorry, Papa. We didn' know we was doin' anythin' wong." Samuel picks her up and sits her down by her sister, whose cheek he then caresses, reassuring her, too.

He squats back down in front of them. "Ah'm not angry with you, girls. Ah just don't trust strangers pokin' 'round our field. Momma an' Ah can't 'ford to lose you, too. Lis'en now. We're gonna stay inside t'nite. Ah'm gonna protect you an' Momma. Keep y'all safe."

"But, Papa," Dorinda begins, "Mr. Ray's a good man. He's kindly tuh us, and Ah don't think he's a bad man at all."

"Yeah, Papa. He's nice," Jamilla adds.

"That may be, hun, but Ah don't know no Mr. Ray. 'Til Ah find out who he is, y'all are gonna stay right here." He pauses for a moment and takes a deep breath. "Now, why don'choo two sit by the fire with Momma?"

Before they can get up, there is a knock at their cabin door. Papa whispers to the girls, "Hide. On th' other side o' the bed, girls." He motions with his hand for them to go. "Now." He stands, places his right hand close to the trigger, and slowly approaches the door. "Who's there?" he asks firmly.

"Mr. Ray," comes a muffled answer.

The girls pop up from behind the bed like prairie dogs. Samuel turns and motions for them to get back down. Gripping the rifle in his right hand and ready for anything, he opens the door slowly with his left and then backs up. He places his left hand on the rifle grip but lowers the barrel. Mr. Ray is standing in the doorway with his hat in his hands. The luminescent glow of the full white moon highlights his grand stature. The girls again jump to their feet in excitement. Their father glances back at them with both surprise and scorn.

"Hello, Samuel, my name is Præsidiel, but please, call me Mr. Ray." He pauses, allowing Samuel to get a good look at him. "May I come in?"

Samuel can see that he is alone and bears no arms. Although he doesn't quite understand why he feels compelled to approve, he reluctantly nods, inviting him to enter. Being tall as he is, Mr. Ray ducks under the doorway. He raises his hands as soon as he crosses the threshold, saying, "Peace be upon this house."

Dorinda and Jamilla cannot stay hidden. They run out excitedly from behind the bed, around their papa, and up to Mr. Ray. Dorinda hugs him around his waist while Jamilla hugs his leg. "We're so glad tuh see yuh, Mr. Ray," Dorinda says.

"Thank you, girls. I am delighted to see you, as well." With a grand smile, he pats Dorinda on the back and Jamilla on the head. They release him and stand staring up at him. Mr. Ray looks at Samuel and points to his rifle. "You will be needing that, Samuel. You have nothing to fear from me."

There is something in his voice as if Samuel has received a command he cannot disobey, yet, at the same time, it pleases his ears and comforts him. A little perplexed, he lowers the barrel of his gun.

Mr. Ray offers a smile of gratitude. "May I greet the mother of the house?" Samuel, still cautiously observing the stranger, silently nods his approval again.

Mr. Ray purposefully but slowly strides to Phiby's side and kneels, facing her. Utterly uninterested in everything transpiring, she continues staring at the fire. Her eyes are dilated and glazed over; there is a sort of incoherence in them. It's as though her heart and mind have retreated to the deepest part of her soul. Mr. Ray places his hand on the bare skin of her forearm, which rests upon the arm of the chair. "Blessed are you who mourn, for you shall be comforted. Peace be upon you, daughter of Eve."

His words call her back from her distant, withdrawn state. Her eyes focus. Phiby turns her gaze from the fire. A look of wonder for Mr. Ray resides in her eyes.

He smiles at her. "There you are, sister."

She looks around the room at her family as though she has just awakened from a deep sleep.

The girls run to her. "Momma!" they say in unison.

Samuel has no words.

Mr. Ray stands and returns to the still-open front door. Awestruck, Samuel watches him like a hawk. He turns to address Samuel. "Will you bring your family and visit me in the field? Again,

I assure you. You have nothing to fear. I promise only healing."

"Ah don't know you, sir," Samuel says cautiously.

"But I know you, Samuel," Mr. Ray answers.

"How can that be?" he asks puzzled.

"Visit me in the field, and all will be revealed. Please bring your queen and your lovely daughters." He winks at the girls. "Dorinda, Jamilla, bring your medicine bottles with you. You will need those." Mr. Ray walks outside onto the porch, puts his hat on his head, and then walks purposefully toward the field.

The girls help their momma up. "C'mon, Papa. Let's go."

He looks at the three of them, disbelieving in what he has just witnessed. Dorinda reassures him, "It'll be all right, Papa. Please, just come with us."

Little Jamilla chimes in, "Yeah, Papa, we got somepin' tuh show yuh. Pwease?" She tilts her head, her wild woolen hair shifts to one side, and she gives him that smile that always melts his heart. Although he knows his daughters are a bit naïve, he sees their deep trust in Mr. Ray. Something within his own heart also tells him he can trust this stranger.

"Okay," he reluctantly agrees.

The girls walk Momma over to Papa. He offers his left arm, and Phiby slides her hand around it. The girls grab their bottles from the bed, run through the door, and bounce off the porch into the sandy front yard. A thin, deep crimson stripe highlights the blackened tree line in the west. The sun has set, and amber and purple hues give way to a dark indigo sky. The stars are beginning to appear in the eastern sky.

Samuel pauses by the table, which is near the door. He sets his rifle down, taking a doubtful second look at it and wondering if he should leave it here. Even though the moonlight illuminates the ground outside, he reaches for the flickering lantern on the table beside his rifle. He then leads Phiby through the door and helps her off the porch. The girls start for the road, but their papa calls to them, "Stay close, girls." They heed his call and dance in the moonlight in front of them with their shiny glass bottles.

The family meets Mr. Ray a couple of minutes later on the road near the field. The girls run up to him again, and he bends to greet them. "Dorinda, Jamilla, you have done well. Thank you." He points to the east, and they look to see the full moon rising just above the tops of the trees. A slight spring breeze stirs the palms and Spanish moss, making them dance in the white light. "You know what the full moon means?" he whispers to them.

"The flowers?" Dorinda asks excitedly.

"Yes. They are blooming right now. But," he cautions, "we must wait for your momma. Remember, all our work was to help her be better."

He stands, holds up his left hand, and greets their parents. "Now, before we go any further, I must ask you a question." An awkward silence replaces the breeze and rattling leaves. "Do you believe in God's love for you?"

"Now that there's an odd thing tuh ask, Mr. Ray," Samuel says.

"Still, do you believe God loves you?"

Phiby has heard the question. It has gone straight to her heart; tears stream uncontrollably from her eyes.

Samuel glances over at her, "Mr. Ray, yer upsettin' her," Samuel retorts anxiously and defensively.

"Samuel, do you believe God loves you?"

Samuel looks at his wife and his children and then lets out a sigh. In his heart, he cannot deny the answer. "Yes. Yes, sir, Ah do believe God loves us." He pauses and then continues, "I jus' don't understand why he took our babies. Why we have tuh suffer like this."

"Samuel. You know scripture, yes?"

"Ah like tuh think Ah do, Mr. Ray."

"Well then, do you remember what Jesus said when his disciples rebuked those who brought little children to him?"

"Yes, sir," Samuel answers humbly. "The Bible tells us Jesus said, 'Suffer little children, 'n forbid 'em not tuh come untuh me: fer such is the kingdom o' heaven.' He then dips his head down, acknowledging the truth of things.

"Very good. Come then," Mr. Ray says in a more cheerful tone. He motions with his hand to follow. "Bring your bride. The girls and I have something for you. Something to brighten your spirits." He smiles at the silent and tear-filled Phiby. The couple respectfully follows.

As they near the edge of the field, they all see a strange glow emanating from it. They round the sabal palm at the corner of the field and observe a blanket of velvety white flowers covering the ground behind their daughters' grave. The vines' dark green and heart-shaped leaves have grown into the semicircle of trees, setting a backdrop for the reflected light of the circular flowers growing in the moonlit alcove. The entire family stops at the entrance to the field. They are amazed by the sheer beauty of it all. Then, as if on cue, tiny golden lights begin to twinkle in the tree line around the edges of the moonflowers.

"What're those?" Dorinda asks, pointing to the blinking lights in amazement.

"Those, child, are fireflies." Mr. Ray kneels between the girls. "They are small beetles whose bellies light up so they can find each other in the dark. Girls, I know darkness can sometimes be scary, but if you carry the light of our Lord in your hearts, you will always be able to find one another in the dark."

"Can Ah catch one?" Jamilla asks playfully.

"Yes. That is why I asked you to bring your bottles." Mr. Ray laughs. "Go ahead. Be gentle when you catch them, though. We have to set them all free before you go back home." Bottles in hand, the girls run about, skipping and jumping around the field, giggling and collecting the blinking fireflies in their bottles. Mr. Ray stands and laughs before turning toward Samuel and Phiby and more serious matters.

As he approaches them, he notices a childlike glimmer in Phiby's eye. He nods at her with a slight smile and motions toward the girls.

"Please, daughter of Eve, dance with your children."

She lets go of Samuel's arm and runs past Mr. Ray into the middle of the field. Holding hands, she dances with Dorinda and Jamilla for a bit before unexpectedly flopping down upon a lush patch of grass in the middle of the field. Samuel starts for her after she flops down, but Mr. Ray holds up his hand, stopping him.

She sits quietly, inspecting the entire field. She sees the grave to her left. Her eye follows the curtain of delicate round flowers, glowing white in the moon's reflection, from the grave to her right, where her girls are catching fireflies. She places her hands behind her, leaning backward and propping herself up. She lifts her head to the large full moon, rising between the oak trees and the tall, skinny pines in the indigo sky. Phiby then turns, looks over her left shoulder at Samuel, and smiles. He sees the life in her again, and his heart leaps with joy. She sits back up and turns to watch her girls dance in the garden.

Mr. Ray now stands to Samuel's right, who is putting his hands into the sides of his overalls. Samuel's brow furls: he is having trouble understanding what is happening. "How?" is all he can get out.

Mr. Ray looks over at him. "Samuel, I asked your daughters this same question: do you know what your name means?"

He keeps his gaze on his wife, children, and the incredible scene unfolding before him. "No, sir, not really. No one ever told me such."

"It means *God has heard*. You were once called Sambo, were you not? That was your slave name, yes?" Samuel snaps his head quickly, looking with fear and astonishment into the blue eyes of Mr. Ray. "I told you, Samuel. I know you. You have forgotten who *you* are, son of Adam? You prayed often when you were a slave, knowing deep in your heart that God would one day be the source of your freedom. Just as he helped the Israelites escape their captivity, you believed he would help you escape too, and so you did."

Mr. Ray turns to look out upon the field. "Instead of fleeing to safety in the Islands of Bahama, however, you stayed here. You joined the Union Army and risked your life to free your brothers and sisters. You served and fought here in this very land. After your service ended, you came back here as a pioneer with other emancipated men, helping to build this community. You have always lived in peace with those native to this land. You have been a devoted husband and a doting father." Mr. Ray pauses for a moment. Letting a grand smile bring slight wrinkles to the corners of his eyes. "Raising two wonderful, innocent, and loving young ladies, I might add."

Mr. Ray turns to look back at Samuel. His eyes are wide and full of water. A single tear breaks free and runs down his weathered ebony face. "How…How do yuh know so much 'bout me, sir?"

"Because I have watched you your whole life."

Samuel is stunned. He cannot grasp how this is possible.

"Samuel, God gave you a strong will, a courageous heart, and a mind anchored in his truth. There is much evil in this world. You know this. You have witnessed its cruelty firsthand. You have been stalked by it and experienced its malevolence. You have been tested as a slave, as a soldier, and now, as a father. You have tasted the bitter fruit of the loss of a child. Through it all, you upheld your oaths to God, your family, and your country. And, though you have suffered much already, you *will* be tested again. When you are, you must accept it courageously and joyfully as you have before. You must be better than those who would persecute you."

Mr. Ray places his left hand on Samuel's shoulder. "Samuel, you once possessed a deep longing for freedom. Freedom from slavery, from tyranny. This is the same freedom the founders of your great country sought. Freedom to speak, worship God, our Father, and travel throughout this gifted land. You wanted to be free to pursue life, liberty, and happiness as they did. You cannot let suffering of any kind harden your heart. Instead, you must be free of the guilt, regret, and despair you carry. You must never forget these things. Our Lord Jesus was also beaten. He, too, stands against the tyranny and oppression of sin. Our Father has felt the sting of having to give his only son up to the cross. There is nothing you have experienced that God has not shared through Jesus, and your faith in him will deliver you and lift you."

Mr. Ray turns again toward the garden, lifting his right hand as if presenting the joyous scene to Samuel anew. Mr. Ray continues, "Besides, God has answered many of your prayers. Look at the gifts you have already been given. You are not alone in your struggles. See, your queen returns to you. You must rediscover the splendor of her heart. See the majesty of this simple garden? You must never overlook the magnificence of Our

Father's creation. See, too, your children dance with delight. Savor the simplicity of their innocent joy. Dwell not on the wounds of your past or the present. Instead, live in the moment with them all." Mr. Ray motions. "Now go. Be with your family in this moment, my friend."

Samuel removes his hands from his overalls and walks swiftly to Phiby's side. He kneels and looks at her soft brown face, which shimmers in the bright moonlight. She meets his gaze, their eyes lock, and their love is rekindled. Phiby smiles again. Genuine peace and happiness shine forth from her copper eyes. Samuel cannot help himself. A smile breaks through his rugged features in response.

He looks about their former picnic spot turned cemetery. It had become a place of mourning and sadness for a time, but the love of his daughters and the kindness of the strange Mr. Ray have transformed it into a place of unbridled splendor.

Jamilla comes running to them, bottle full of fireflies in hand. She holds them up proudly. "Look what Ah caught, Momma!" she exclaims, short of breath.

Samuel chuckles, and Phiby smiles at her.

"You like them moonflowers, Momma?" she asks with a big grin. Jamilla can see the happiness on her mother's face and knows her pain is gone.

"Oh, mah darlin', yes. Yes, Ah do," Phiby says softly and lovingly.

Dorinda hears her momma's pleasant voice and comes running. She falls to her knees on the grass in front of her. Phiby reaches out to them both and embraces them. "Mah beautiful babies. Now Ah have mornin' glories an' moonflowers. Yuh know Ah love yuh both. Ah'm so sorry for what Ah put y'all through."

"S'okay, Momma. Me 'n Dorinda, we knew you wasn't feelin' good. That's why we helped Mr. Ray grow them flowers. He said they'd make yuh feel better," Jamilla says. Dorinda sniffles and wipes a tear away with her sleeve while still holding her bottle of flashing golden fireflies.

"Ah know, girls. Ah'm so grateful. Yuh'll never know jus' how proud momma is of you." Phiby looks upon them with renewed love.

From behind them, near the entrance to the alcove, Mr. Ray speaks, "It is time for me to go. Before I do, though, I have one more gift for you."

Samuel helps Phiby up, and the whole family stands and faces him. As he approaches them, his appearance begins to change. "I offer you the gift of sight." A bright white light burns away the appearance of the road-weary traveler, revealing his true angelic form. The light subsides, and his brilliant white wings spread upward behind him. He is wearing deep blue Romanesque armor over a light gray tunic. His belt and sandals are gold in color. At his side is his gladius in a golden sheath.

A golden-colored halo around his head replaces the hat he wore.

Samuel and Phiby instantly kneel. Dorinda sees this and also kneels. "Ah knew it!" Jamilla exclaims, still standing. She takes her right hand off the bottle top to point at Præsidiel, and two of her fireflies escape. "Ah knew you was an angel." She jumps up and down, squealing with giddiness before realizing the rest of her fireflies are escaping.

Præsidiel smiles warmly at her and lifts his hands upward and outward as he nears them, instructing, "Rise. Please, stand. You need not kneel to me, only to our Lord Jesus." Then, he smiles, placing his left hand on Samuel's right shoulder and his right on Phiby's shoulder. "Samuel, I have always known you because I am your guardian angel. I look forward to keeping you and your beautiful family safe in the coming days. That said, I know you are not without grief; you both have much healing to do. However, the Lord sends you this gift. He knows this will bring you peace in your moments of sorrow."

A vision appears in their minds. Two baby girls, wrapped in pure white swaddling clothes, rest in the arms of Christ Jesus. He is seated with them on his lap. He looks upon them with great love while they coo in response. Their chubby, light brown cheeks reflect the light of his face. He gently kisses each child on the forehead. A booming yet soft voice reverberates through their hearts, minds, and entire beings. "Do not worry. You will see them again. Until then, no harm shall ever come to them. They will be safe and loved forever."

The vision ends as swiftly as it came. Their hearts pound within their chests; both exhilaration and peace overcome them. Their eyes glaze over with tears. Neither Samuel nor Phiby will ever forget hearing the Lord's sweet, powerful voice. The sight of his radiant face, as he blessed Jemima and Sabina with a kiss, will neither be erased from their thoughts.

Their worldly sight returns, and Præsidiel is standing in front of them again. He smiles at them all. "Remember, trust in the Lord. Rejoice and be happy. Have courage. Be bold. Forgive those who cannot see beyond your skin into your blessed hearts. Build a better future for yourselves and your children, and never forget to love." He begins to beat his wings, slowly lifting himself upward into the night sky. "Farewell, my friends. We shall meet again." The angel waves a final time before rising slowly into the night sky.

Then, as swift as a streaking star, he blazes out of sight and into the heavens.

Laughter, forgotten over the last few weeks, returns. Samuel once again sees the spark of life in Phiby's chestnut eyes. Mother and daughters celebrate their beautiful garden of lights. Dorinda and Jamilla showed their momma how to catch moonbeams in their bottles and how they fed their twining vines. They teach their papa the blessing Mr. Ray taught them. Parents and children alike laugh and dance in the moonlit garden. The family is reborn in majesty, happiness, and love that night.

Epilogue: God Will Hear

Summer has come and gone; it's now early fall, and although it's late morning, it is still a bit hot outside. Nevertheless, the South Florida weather is still beautiful. Phiby has fully recovered and is back to her happy, hardworking self. She and the girls have thoroughly cleaned the cabin and helped grow a fruitful garden nearly ready for harvesting.

It's Saturday, and Samuel has a rare day off. Most of his chores are already done, so he takes a break in the porch shade. Phiby steps out through the front door and calls back to their daughters, "You young'uns keep grindin' up all that allspice. When yer done with that, Ah want yuh to start churnin' that cream. Papa 'n Ah are goin' for a walk. Stay in the house 'til we get back."

"We are?" asks a surprised Samuel.

Phiby gives him a coy glance and smiles. "When we get back, Ah promise we'll all go for a carriage ride in tuh town. Maybe get some fresh bread tuh go with that butter yer churnin'."

"We will?" Samuel rebuffs quietly.

"Okay, Momma!" the girls shout excitedly.

Phiby struts over to Samuel and playfully takes his hand. She leads him off the porch and starts down the road to the field, continuing to hold his hand as they go. "You seem quite happy today," Samuel remarks.

"Oh, Ah am, mah love. Ah am." A sort of mischievous smile spreads across her beautiful face. Once they round the corner from the cabin and are on the open road, Phiby releases Samuel's hand, picks up her dress, and starts to run. She glances playfully over her shoulder at him, laughing. He smiles grandly and begins to pursue her. He quickly catches up to her, grabbing her by the waist. They both laugh as young lovers would. They stop for a kiss right before they enter the alcove. The expansive growth of the moonflower vines, which now cover the back of the field like a rich, dark green blanket, never fails to mesmerize. Samuel looks around while Phiby keeps her gaze on him. A light breeze moves through the treetops, and the late morning sun makes the shadows dance on the field.

"You 'member that day, Samuel? When we was young? When we took our lunch in this field?"

"Yes, ma'am, Ah do." He pauses. "Seems even more beautiful now."

Phiby moves in front of Samuel and rests her arms on his shoulders, clasping her hands around the back of his neck. There is a twinkle in her eye that Samuel hasn't seen for some time. "More beautiful than me?" she asks seductively.

"No, mah queen. Nuthin's more beautiful than you."

She raises to kiss him on the lips. Samuel places his hands on her hips and returns her kiss. A loving fire is ignited. Their kisses become deeper, more passionate. Phiby pulls away slightly. Keeping her hands on his shoulders, she walks backward, slowly leading him toward the moonflower vines. Eventually, seeing them at her feet, she stops. She begins to sway her hips, dancing and coxing Samuel to swing around to where she is. Once his back is toward the vines, she slides her hands from around his neck down to his chest and unbuckles his overalls. She lets them go, and they fall to the ground. She then playfully pushes him down on the thick blanket of moonflower vines. There, resting on his elbows, he watches his seductive wife.

Phiby undoes the buttons on the front of her dress. She slowly removes her arms from the dress and then lets it fall to the ground. With her eyes fixed on Samuel, she steps over her clothing, displaying both the naked, natural, and utterly vulnerable beauty to her beloved. He is captivated by her soft curves and delicate brown skin. With slow, seductive movements, she approaches him, lowering herself over him. Samuel's passion swells. With the lightest touch, she invites him to enter. She envelopes him, and he embraces her. In the late afternoon summer sun, on a bed of moonflower vines, husband and wife consummate their love with a burning passion unfelt for some time. The two once again become one in body, mind, and soul. They give themselves to each other, without reservation, until they are both entirely spent.

Exhausted and out of breath, they fall back into the lush vines. Lying side by side for a time, they feel a deep connection that goes beyond the physical body. A unifying love for one another that comes from deep within their souls. The love, the passion, the unending possibilities of a life bound together as soul mates surge within their beating hearts.

Phiby rests her head on Samuel's right shoulder. He gazes skyward, watching small white clouds move across the bright blue sky while running his fingertips up and down Phiby's naked side. He delights in the softness of her bare skin. That moment reminds him of the day they were united in marriage and when they made love for the first time.

He never felt more complete that day. So many past fears and trials were behind him, and with her at his side, a bright future lay before them. He knew he could not be without her from the day he met her. Now, once again, she lies on her left side with her arm draped across his broad chest.

Phiby reaches up to touch his face before sliding her right leg over his. She lets out a sigh and a moan. "Mmmm…Samuel, Ah love you."

"An' Ah love you, mah queen."

"Thank you, mah love," she whispers in his ear. "Thank you for never givin' up on me."

Samuel turns his head to look into her chestnut eyes. "Ah never will, Phiby. Ah never will."

She tilts her head up. His lips met her full, soft lips in a slow, lasting kiss.

* * * * *

A few weeks later, Samuel is reclining at the dinner table, staring at his beautiful bride and darling daughters as they prepare Sunday dinner. He sometimes sits and watches them; he is reminded of all he has come through and is thankful for all he has been blessed with. He focuses on Phiby. Something is different. She has let her loosely curled hair down with only a kerchief, keeping it out of her face. She is leaning over, happily and patiently instructing Dorinda and Jamilla how to make one of Papa's favorite meals. When she stands upright and turns, he suddenly realizes what is different about her. He sits up promptly in his surprise, lovingly calling to her. "Come 'ere, Phiby."

She glides across the cabin with that playful grin on her glowing face and, in a fluid, graceful motion, wraps her right arm around his shoulders and sits on his lap. "Yes, mah love?" she says with a twinkle in her eyes.

Samuel gently but firmly places his open palm on her belly. It feels bigger and rounder. He smiles and looks up at her. The radiant glow from her soft brown face seems to brighten. "Is this…?" He begins.

Phiby nods yes. "Yes, it is." She smiles. "God has blessed us again."

Dorinda knows that look; she's heard those words before. She leans down and whispers something to Jamilla. Then a sudden squeal erupts from Jamilla, "Eeeeeeee!" Both girls run toward their momma and papa, throwing their arms around their parents. Jamilla, possessing no subtlety, blurts out, "You gonna have another baby, Momma?"

"Yes, mah li'l mornin' glories. Yer gonna be big sisters again."

A sudden and unexpected sting of apprehension clouds Samuel's mind. A voice, whispering and malevolent, tries to implant fear in his mind. "Do you think this child will survive? Can you be sure it will not suffer?" Samuel quickly rebukes the voice. *Ah, have no fear,* he thought to himself. He knows he can trust God in all things; he has faith in his divine providence. The voice and doubt leave him. A sense of peace falls upon his heart, and another firm, familiar voice speaks softly, "Do not worry, Samuel. Do not fear. Everything is going to be just fine." He looks at his bride's glowing face and his daughters' beaming smiles, and he believes it to be true—that everything will be okay.

* * * * *

Winter has passed. A small gathering of friends and neighbors is in the spring air outside a simple log cabin. A crowd of different people has come together: carpenters, nurses, merchants, farmers, ranchers, and even a few remaining Seminoles. They have come together for a family they love and respect. All their children play in the grass on the side of the cabin with the girls who live there. There is much excitement, anticipation, and cheer in the air. The people happily converse with one another while awaiting a big announcement.

A newborn's cry pierces the cabin walls, spurring the crowd to a hush. Minutes later, a strong, weathered man in his early thirties moves toward the front door. This man was once a fearless slave who became a courageous soldier and then a bold pioneer. Now, he lives life as a well-known and trusted carpenter, a loving husband, a doting father, and a friend to the community. The man crosses the threshold out onto the porch. He walks with a slow, confident demeanor, that of a free Christian man secure in his faith. Although he usually walks with his head and back upright, today, he walks with his head down. He whispers to a small swaddled bundle warmly cradled in his arms, "Oh, mah precious son. How long Ah have waited for yuh. Because

Ah know God will hear you as he heard me. Ah give yuh the name Ishmael."

Samuel raises his eyes to see his friends who have gathered to welcome Ishmael into the world.

The End

About the Author

John Eudy is a 26-year military veteran. He was a soldier in the Army National Guard and a 'shallow water' sailor in the U.S. Coast Guard.

Admittedly not as well-traveled as the wayfarer rat, he has at least been up and down the river a time or two. Additional expeditions include cautiously wandering the lava fields of Kilauea, snowshoeing to the summit of Cadillac Mountain, strolling among giants in King's Canyon, and swimming with wild dolphins in the Gulf of America (which he embarrassingly thought were sharks at first sight). John even traveled through time once … by making a roundtrip across the international date line to visit Guam.

These days, John and his family reside smack-dab in the middle of the country, not too far from the river, though. He has been married to his lovely wife of 30 years, and they are the proud parents of four daughters, two of whom are already with God in heaven.

Inspired by faith and scripture, he enjoys weaving history, cultural legends, personal life experiences, and Christian morality into fictional novellas.